*All children have
a great ambition to read
to themselves...*

*and a sense of achievement when they can do so.
The* **read it yourself** *series has been devised to
satisfy their ambition. Since many children learn
from the Ladybird Key Words Reading Scheme,
these stories have been based to a large extent
on the Key Words List, and the tales chosen are
those with which children are likely to be familiar.*

*The series can of course be used as
supplementary reading for any reading scheme.
Three Little Pigs is intended for children reading
up to Book 3c of the Ladybird Reading Scheme.
The following words are additional to the
vocabulary used at that level –*

little, big, pig, new, not, bad, wolf,
make, straw, house, two, sticks,
bricks, roof, of, let, huff, puff,
blow, eats, hot, splash, soup

*A list of other titles at the same level will be
found on the back cover.*

Three Little Pigs

by Fran Hunia
illustrated by Kathie Layfield

Ladybird Books Loughborough

Here are the little pigs.

They are at home
with Mummy pig.

You are getting big,
says Mummy pig.
You have to go
to look for a new home.

Yes, say the little pigs.

We can look for a new home.

Mummy pig
gives the little pigs
some apples
and some cakes.

See that the big bad wolf
can not get you,
says Mummy pig.

The little pigs go
to look for a new home.

They see a man.

The man has some straw.

One little pig says,
Please give me some straw.
I want to make a new home.

Yes, says the man.

Here is some straw for you.

You can make a good house
with straw.

He gives the little pig
some straw.

The little pig makes a house.

A rabbit comes to look at it.

I like that house,
says the rabbit.

Yes, says the little pig.
It is a good house.
You can play here with me.
The wolf can not get in here.

Two little pigs go on.

They see a man
with some sticks.

One little pig says,
Please give me some sticks.
I want to make a new home.

Yes, says the man.

Here are some sticks for you.

You can make a good house
with sticks.

He gives the little pig
some sticks.

The little pig makes a house.

I like this house,

he says.

I have flowers and trees

to look at.

I can have fun here.

The big bad wolf

can not get me.

One little pig goes on.

He sees a man
with some bricks.

Please give me some bricks,
says the little pig.
I want to make a new home.

Yes, says the man.

Here are some bricks

for you.

You can make a good house

with bricks.

He gives the little pig

some bricks.

The little pig makes
a good house.

It has a red roof.

He is pleased with it.

I can play in this house,
he says.
The big bad wolf
can not get me.

Here is the big bad wolf.

He looks at the little pig
in the house of straw.

I can get that little pig,
he says.

The wolf goes up
to the house of straw.

He says,
Little pig, little pig,
let me come in.

No, no, says the little pig.
I can not let you in.

I can huff,

I can puff,

I can blow the house down,

says the wolf.

He huffs and he puffs.

Help, help,

says the little pig.

Down comes

the house of straw.

The wolf eats up

the little pig.

The wolf goes up
to the house of sticks.

He says,
Little pig, little pig,
let me come in.

No, no, says the little pig.
I can not let you in.

I can huff,

I can puff,

I can blow the house down,

says the wolf.

He huffs and he puffs.

Help, help,

says the little pig.

Down comes

the house of sticks.

The wolf eats up

the little pig.

The wolf goes up

to the house of bricks.

He says,

Little pig, little pig,

let me come in.

No, no, says the little pig.

I can not let you in.

41

I can huff,

I can puff,

I can blow the house down,

says the wolf.

He huffs and he puffs.

He goes red.

He huffs and he puffs.

He gets redder and redder.

The house of bricks
is a good house.

The wolf can not
blow it down.

The wolf is not pleased.

He jumps up and down.

I can get that little pig,
he says.

He gets up on the roof.

The little pig

is making some soup.

The soup is hot.

The wolf comes down

SPLASH

into the hot soup.

The little pig is pleased.

The house of straw
was not good.

The house of sticks
was not good.

The house of bricks
is a good house.

I like it here,
says the little pig.